For Joe

JANETTA OTTER-BARRY BOOKS

First published in Great Britain and the USA in 2010
by Frances Lincoln Children's Books, 4 Torriano Mews,
Torriano Avenue, London NW5 2RZ

www.franceslincoln.com

A catalogue record for this book is available from the British Library.

ISBN 978-1-84507-988-8

Illustrated with collage and watercolour

Printed in Dongguan, Guangdong, China by Toppan Leefung in May 2010

1 3 5 7 9 8 6 4 2

Ahmed
and the
Feather Girl

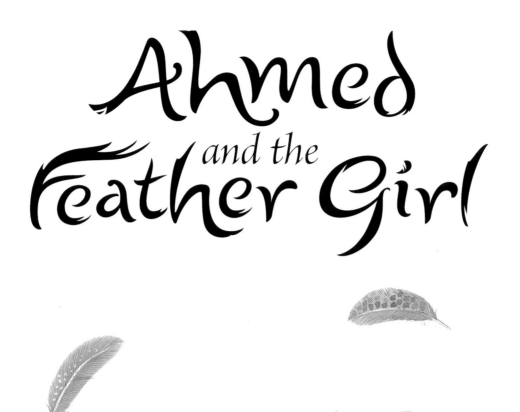

Jane Ray

FRANCES LINCOLN
CHILDREN'S BOOKS

There was once a little orphan boy with big dark eyes.
He was called Ahmed and he lived with a travelling circus.
The circus was owned by an old woman called
Madame Saleem who was cruel and bad-tempered.
Ahmed was afraid of her.

She made Ahmed work very hard. He fetched firewood
and carried water. He swept out caravans and fed the animals.
He washed the clothes and cooked the food.

At night he huddled near the embers of the dying
camp fire and stared up at the stars, until he fell asleep.

One winter's day, Ahmed was picking up firewood
in the forest. As he wandered, he came across
a golden egg lying in the middle of the path.
Where could it have come from?

Ahmed worried that the egg would get cold lying
in the snow, so he carefully carried it back to the circus.
He made a nest of willow branches close to the fire
to keep it warm.

When Madame Saleem saw the golden egg she grew
very excited. She snatched it up and locked it away in
a golden cage.

From a distance, Ahmed kept a careful watch on the egg.

Spring came, and the days grew warmer.

One morning, Ahmed heard a cracking sound. The egg was hatching! He watched in amazement as the egg opened to reveal a beautiful little child. She uncurled her limbs, opened her big, dark eyes and smiled straight at Ahmed.

The circus people named the little girl Aurelia.
Her hair was as soft as feathers, her eyes sparkled,
and each morning, as the sun came up,
she sang and sang.

When Madame Saleem saw the little child, she danced
with delight. "We'll put her on show!" she cried.

Everywhere the circus went, people queued up to see
The Girl Hatched From a Golden Egg.

Madame Saleem counted in the money…

The Girl Hatched
From a Golden Egg

Weeks went by and the circus moved on.
   The little girl began to change and grow.
Tiny points appeared on her back and began to sprout
fine silken feathers.
   The more beautiful Aurelia became, the more people
came to see her. The more people who came to see her,
the more money Madame Saleem counted in.

And every night, when he had finished his chores,
Ahmed lay down next to the golden cage, and he
and Aurelia stared up at the stars until they fell asleep.

But as spring turned to summer, Aurelia grew unhappy. She could hear the forest birds calling to her. She longed to be able to spread her new wings and fly up into the sky.

Ahmed knew that he must free her – but how could he get hold of the key to the golden cage? By day it hung on a cord around Madame Saleem's neck and at night she slept with it under her pillow.

One day Aurelia stopped singing altogether, and Ahmed
knew he had to act. That night, he summoned up all his courage
and crept into Madame Saleem's caravan, where she lay snoring
in her bunk. Holding his breath, he slid his hand under her
pillow and found the key.

Ahmed ran out to the golden cage
and unlocked the door.

Aurelia felt the night breeze ruffling her feathers
and heard the nightingales calling. For the first time,
she could open her wings. With a deep breath
and a burst of song she flew up into the night sky.
    Ahmed watched until she was just a speck amongst
the stars…

Ahmed ran to put the key back. But the rickety old caravan creaked as he crept in and Madame Saleem opened one eye. She shrieked and leapt out of bed, chasing Ahmed outside.

When she saw the golden cage was empty, Madame Saleem exploded with rage.

Ahmed hid under one of the caravans and wept.
He was happy that Aurelia was free, but now he
would never see her again, and he felt lonelier than ever.
He cried himself to sleep, and he dreamed of Aurelia.
In his dream she plucked from her wing a soft feather
that floated down and brushed his cheek. Then, without
a sound, she was gone – but when Ahmed woke in the
morning, there was the feather clasped in his hand.

Madame Saleem made Ahmed work even harder as punishment for setting Aurelia free. Now he had only crusts and scraps to eat, and he slept huddled under a caravan. He was cold and hungry, and he missed Aurelia.

But each night he had the same dream, and each morning he awoke holding more feathers. He collected them in his tattered old blanket and kept them safe. They helped him remember Aurelia.

Summer passed and autumn came.
It was time for the circus to move closer to town.
Everything was packed up and the circus trundled
on its way.

One snowy night, as he lay shivering, Ahmed heard the most beautiful singing.

There, perched on the caravan roof, was Aurelia!

"Put on your feathers, Ahmed – it`s time to go!" she sang.

And Ahmed saw that all the feathers Aurelia had brought him in his dreams had become a soft, warm cloak of pink and grey, gold and amber.

He pulled the cloak around him. It fitted perfectly.

Aurelia took Ahmed`s hand and gave it a little tug.
Ahmed found himself rising above the circus,
above the town.

He took a deep breath and leaned into the wind.

Together, Ahmed and Aurelia
flew through the snowflakes,
up into the dark night sky,
to the place beyond
the stars.